There is no one method or technique that is the ONLY way to learn to read. Children learn in a variety of ways. **Read with me** is an enjoyable and uncomplicated scheme that will give your child reading confidence. Through exciting stories about Kate, Tom and Sam the dog, **Read with me**:

- *teaches the first 300 key words (75% of our everyday language) plus 500 additional words*

- *stimulates a child's language and imagination through humorous, full colour illustration*

- *introduces situations and events children can relate to*

- *encourages and develops conversation and observational skills*

- *support material includes Practice and Play Books, Flash Cards, Book and Cassette Packs*

Always praise and encourage as you go along. Keep your reading sessions short and stop immediately if your child loses interest.

Published by Ladybird Books Ltd
27 Wrights Lane London W8 5TZ
A Penguin Company
3 5 7 9 10 8 6 4

Printed in Italy

Read with me
First Words
a pre-reader

by WILLIAM MURRAY
compiled by JILL CORBY
illustrated by CHRIS RUSSELL

Kate

Tell the story.

What will happen next?

Tom

Tell the story.

What will happen next?

Sam

Tell the story.

Where is Sam's bone?

Dad

Mum

Friends

John

Suki

Lucy

Here is Tom.

Under a stone where the earth
                    was firm,
Tom found a wiggly, wriggly worm.
"Good morning," he said.
"How are you today?"
But the wiggly worm just
                    wriggled away.

Here is Kate.

Which is different?

Which two are the same?

Tell this story.

Find these pictures in the story.

Talk about the picture.

How many things of each colour can you count?

Tell the story.

Do you know this story?

Talk about this picture.
Which animals are watching
Little Red Riding Hood?

What belongs to Kate, John, Suki and Tom?

Which one is different in each row?

Talk about this picture.
Where is Sam?

How many mice can you find?

Kate and Tom
like the ball.

Find six differences in this picture.

LADYBIRD
READING SCHEMES

Ladybird reading schemes are suitable for use
with any other method of learning to read.

Say the Sounds

Ladybird's **Say the Sounds** graded reading scheme is a
phonics scheme. It teaches children the sounds of individual
letters and letter combinations, enabling them to tackle new
words by building them up as a blend of smaller units.

There are 8 titles in this scheme:

1 **Rocket to the jungle**   5 **Humpty Dumpty and the robots**
2 **Frog and the lollipops**   6 **Flying saucer**
3 **The go-cart race**   7 **Dinosaur rescue**
4 **Pirate's treasure**   8 **The accident**

Support material available: Practice Books, Double Cassette Pack,
Flash Cards